PADDINGTON'S
PICTURE
BOOK

William Collins Sons & Co Ltd
London · Glasgow · Sydney · Auckland
Toronto · Johannesburg

This edition published 1979 by Book Club Associates
by arrangement with Wm. Collins, Sons & Co. Ltd.

For older children Michael Bond has written
ten Paddington story books, all illustrated
by Peggy Fortnum.

Made and Printed in Great Britain by
William Collins Sons & Co Ltd Glasgow

Paddington's
Picture Book

MICHAEL BOND AND
FRED BANBERY

BOOK CLUB ASSOCIATES
LONDON

Contents

Here, for the first time under one cover, is a bumper
edition of all six Paddington Picture Books. (Complete
with his special paw-mark to show they are genuine!)

From then on it's but a short bear's stride away from
"mishaps" in the garden, "disasters" in the super-market,
"dramas" at the circus, and "goings-on" at the sea-side.
But as with all Paddington's adventures, things turn out
happily in the end — even when he rounds things off by
having a strange encounter with some ravens at the
Tower of London.

In short, it's the sort of book which would strike
Paddington himself as being very good value indeed; and
that in itself makes it a "must" for young bears
everywhere, not to mention their hordes of faithful
admirers.

Originally written with young readers in mind, the
stories begin at the beginning with the tale of how
Paddington came to live with the Browns at No. 32
Windsor Gardens.

Paddington
Bear

One day Mr and Mrs Brown were standing in
Paddington Station. They were waiting for their
daughter Judy who was coming home from
school. Suddenly Mr Brown noticed something
small and furry behind a pile of mailbags.

"Look over there," he said to Mrs Brown,
"I'm sure I saw a bear."

"A *bear*?" said Mrs Brown. "On Paddington
station? Don't be silly, Henry. There can't be."

But there was. It had a funny kind of hat and
it was sitting all by itself on an old suitcase near
the Lost Property Office.

As they drew near, the bear stood up and politely raised its hat. "Good afternoon," it said, in a small clear voice. "Can I help you?"

"We were wondering if *we* could help *you*," said Mrs Brown. "Where ever have you come from?"

The bear looked round carefully before replying. "*Darkest* Peru. I stowed away and I lived on marmalade!"

Mrs Brown spied a label round the bear's neck. It said simply: PLEASE LOOK AFTER THIS BEAR. THANK YOU. AUNT LUCY.

"Henry," she exclaimed, "we shall have to take him home with us."

"But we don't even know his name," began Mr Brown.

"We'll call him Paddington," said Mrs Brown.
"Because that's where we found him."

Mrs Brown went off to look for Judy and
Mr Brown took Paddington into the buffet for
something to eat.

He left Paddington sitting at a corner table near the window. He soon returned carrying two steaming cups of tea and a large plate piled high with sticky cakes.

After his long journey Paddington felt so
hungry and thirsty he didn't know which to
do first – eat or drink.

"I think I'll try both at the same time if you
don't mind, Mr Brown," he announced.

And without waiting for a reply he climbed up onto the table. Mr Brown stared out of the window, pretending he had tea with a bear at Paddington station every day of his life.

When Mrs Brown came into the buffet with Judy she threw up her hands in horror.

"Henry," she said. "What *are* you doing to that poor bear? He's covered all over with cream and jam."

At the sound of Mrs Brown's voice Paddington
jumped so much he stepped on a patch of
strawberry jam and fell over backwards into
his saucer of tea.

"I think we'd better go before anything else
happens," said Mr Brown. And he quickly led
the way out of the buffet.

Judy took Paddington's paw and squeezed it.

"Come along," she said. "We'll take you home in a taxi. Then you can have a nice hot bath and meet my brother Jonathan."

Paddington had never been in a taxi before.
He found it very exciting and he stood on a

little tip-up seat behind the driver so that he could wave to the people in the street.

Soon they pulled up outside a large house with a green front door.

When they were indoors Judy took Paddington up to his room to unpack.

"I haven't got very much," said Paddington. "Only some marmalade. . .

. . . and my scrapbook . . .

. . . and a sort of South American penny."

He held up
a photograph.
"And that's my
Aunt Lucy.
She had it taken
just before she went
into the Home for
Retired Bears."

Next Judy showed Paddington to the bathroom.

As soon as he was on his own he turned on the taps and then climbed onto a stool in order to look out of the window.

Then he tried writing his name on the steamy glass with his paw. It took him rather a long time and when he looked round he found to his surprise that the bath was so full of water it was starting to run over the side.

He closed his eyes, and, holding his nose with one paw, he jumped in.

The water was hot, soapy, and very deep,
and to his horror he found he couldn't get out.
He couldn't even see to turn the taps off.

Paddington tried calling out "Help"; at first
in a quiet voice, so as not to disturb anyone
and then much louder, "HELP! HELP!"

But still nobody came.

Then he had an idea.

He took off his hat and began using it to
bale out the water.

Downstairs, Judy was telling her brother all about Paddington.

Suddenly, she felt a PLOP.

Looking up she saw a dark, wet patch on the ceiling.

"Paddington!" she cried. "He must be in trouble. Quick!"

And together they raced out of the room.

Jonathan and Judy leant over the side of the
bath and lifted a dripping and very frightened
Paddington on to the floor.

"What a mess!" said Jonathan. "We'd better
wipe it up pretty quickly."

"Oh Paddington," said Judy. "What a good job we found you in time. You might have drowned."

Paddington sat up. "What a good job I had my hat," he said.

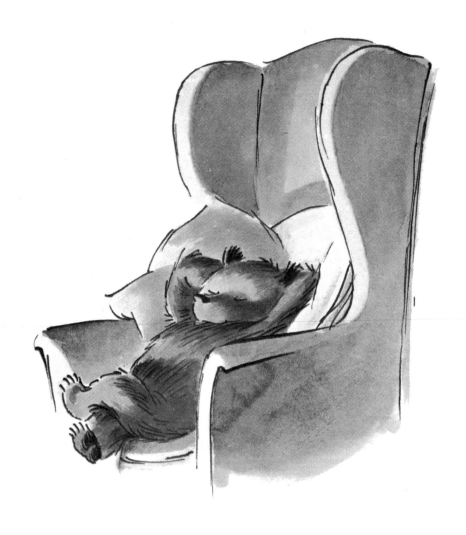

Some time later a beautifully clean Paddington
came downstairs. Settling himself down in a
small armchair by the fire, he put his paws
behind his head and stretched out his toes.

It was nice being a bear – especially a bear
called Paddington. He had a feeling that life
with the Browns was going to be fun.

Paddington's Garden

One day Paddington decided to make a list of all
the nice things there were about being a bear
and living with the Browns at number thirty-two
Windsor Gardens.

It was a long list and he had almost reached the
end of the paper when he suddenly realized
he'd left out one of the nicest things of all . . .
the garden itself!

Paddington liked the Browns' garden. It was
quiet and peaceful, and there were times when it
might not have been in London at all.

But nice gardens usually mean a lot of hard work, and after a day at his office Mr Brown often wished it wasn't quite so large.

It was Mrs Brown who first thought of giving
Jonathan, Judy and Paddington a piece each of
their own.

"It will keep them out of mischief," she said.

"And it will help you at the same time."

So Mr Brown marked out three squares, and to make it more exciting he said he would give a prize to whoever had the best idea.

Early next morning all three set to work.

Judy thought she would grow some flowers, and Jonathan started to make a paved garden, but Paddington didn't know what to do.

Gardening was much harder than it looked —
especially with paws, and he soon grew tired of
digging.

In the end he decided to do some shopping.
He had some savings left over from his pocket
money and he bought a wheelbarrow, a trowel,

and a large packet of assorted seeds.
It seemed very good value indeed—especially
as he still had two pence left over.

The shopkeeper told him that when planning a new garden it was a good idea to stand some way away first in order to picture what it would look like when it was finished. So, taking a jar of his best chunky marmalade, Paddington set out to visit the nearby building site.

By the time he got there it was the middle of the morning, and as the men were all at their tea break he sat down on a pile of bricks, put the

jar of marmalade on a wooden platform for
safety, and then peered hopefully towards the
Browns' garden.

After sitting there for some while without getting
a single idea Paddington decided to try taking a
short walk instead.

When he got back his eyes nearly popped out.
A man was emptying the concrete mixer on
the very spot where he'd left his jar of chunky
marmalade!

At that moment the foreman came round the corner and seeing the look on Paddington's face he stopped to ask what was wrong.

Paddington pointed to the pile of wet cement.
"All my chunks have been buried!" he
exclaimed hotly.

The foreman called his men together. "There's a young bear gentleman here who's lost some very valuable chunks," he said urgently.

They set to work clearing the cement.

Soon the ground was covered with small piles, but still there was no sign of Paddington's jar.

Suddenly there was a whirring sound from somewhere overhead and to Paddington's surprise a platform landed at his feet.

"My marmalade!" he exclaimed thankfully.

"Your marmalade?" echoed the foreman, staring at the jar. "Did you say *marmalade*?"

"That's right," said Paddington. "I put it there ready for my tea break. It must have been taken up by mistake."

It was the foreman's turn to look as if he could
hardly believe his eyes.

"That's special quick-drying cement!" he
wailed. "It's probably going rock-hard already—

ruined by a bear's marmalade! No one will give me two pence for it now!''

Paddington opened his suitcase and felt in the secret compartment. ''I will,'' he said eagerly.

Paddington took the lumps of concrete home in his wheelbarrow and worked hard in his garden for the rest of the day. When the builders saw the rockery he had made with the concrete they were most impressed and gave Paddington several plants to finish it off for the time being...

. . . until his seeds started to grow.

Paddington's rockery fitted in so well with
Jonathan's paved garden and Judy's flower bed
it looked as though the whole thing had been
planned.

Mr Brown was so pleased he decided to give
them all an extra week's pocket money, and that
evening they celebrated by having tea in the
new garden.

After it was over Paddington stayed on for a while in order to finish off his list of all the nice things there were about being a bear and living at number thirty-two Windsor Gardens.

He had one more important item to add.

MY ROCKERY

Then he signed his name and added his special paw print . . .

. . . just to show it was genuine.

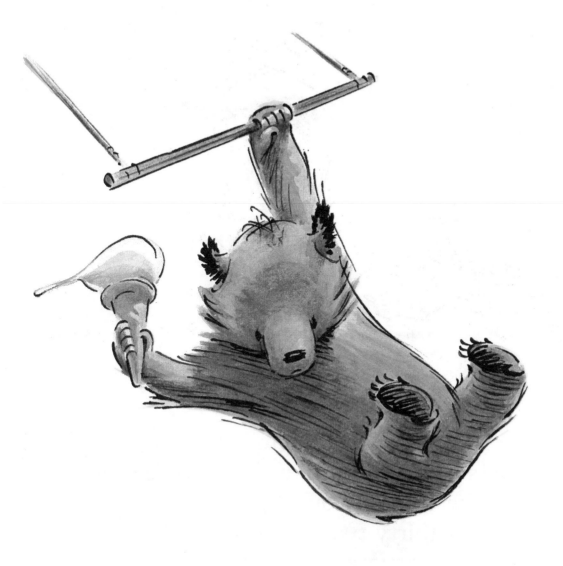

Paddington
at the Circus

One day Paddington was out doing his morning shopping when he came across a very strange-looking man pasting a picture to a wall.

It showed a huge tent decorated with red and green and blue lights and streamers and across the middle were the words – THE GREATEST SHOW ON EARTH. ONE NIGHT ONLY. BOOK NOW.

When Paddington got home he hurried indoors
to tell the others.

"The Greatest Show on Earth?" repeated
Jonathan, giving Judy a wink. "In a *tent*? You

must have been dreaming!"

Then Judy announced the good news. It was a
circus and they all had tickets for the front row
that very evening.

Paddington had never been to a circus before and he grew more and more excited as the time drew near.

The lights were already on when they arrived and there was a lovely smell of sawdust in the air. It looked very gay and inviting.

But the circus itself was even more exciting.

There was a band, and a Ring-master in a top hat, and even a lady selling ice-creams.

Altogether there was so much to see Paddington didn't know what to look at first.

"I think I would like to join a circus, Mr Brown," he announced happily.

Then he caught sight of
the man he had met
that morning.
He was in the
middle of the ring,
balancing a bucket
on the end of
a long pole.
"That's a clown,"
explained Judy.
"He's standing
on stilts. That's
why he looks
so tall."

Paddington waved and
the man came over
and bent down to shake
his paw. The bucket
tipped, and Paddington
jumped up in alarm.

Luckily the bucket was empty and it was tied to the end of the pole, so Paddington soon got over his fright.

Mr Brown bought him an ice-cream and as the band started to play they sat back to enjoy the show. All, that is, except Paddington.

The first act was hardly over when he had yet another shock. Looking up towards the roof of the tent he saw a man hanging from a rope.

"I expect that's one of the Popular Prices," began Jonathan, looking at the programme. "They are trapeze artists . . ."

But Paddington didn't stop to listen. "Don't worry, Mr Price," he called. "I'm coming!"

Before the others could stop him Paddington was halfway up the nearest tent pole.

He clambered on to a small platform and then

nearly fell off again with surprise when he saw
a second man coming towards him.

He was dressed in tights and was riding a bicycle.

But Paddington was not nearly as surprised as the men themselves.

"Look out!" shouted the leader. "Hold on!"

Paddington did as he was told. He grabbed the nearest thing he could see.

It came away in his paw and the next moment
he found himself flying through the air.

The audience had been clapping before, but when Paddington appeared they clapped more loudly than ever, for they all thought he was part of the act.

He missed the platform on the other side and began to swing backwards and forwards, getting lower and lower, until he came to a stop over the middle of the ring.

"Don't let go!" shouted the Ring-master. "Whatever you do – don't let go!"

And then he stopped and a look of horror came over his face as something soft and white landed on his beautifully brushed top hat.

"Crikey!" exclaimed Jonathan. "Paddington's ice cream!"

In the end it was Paddington's
friend, the clown who saved him.
He held up the bucket on the
end of his pole so that Paddington
could step into it.

The cheers as he landed in the ring made the whole tent shake.

"Best act I've seen in years!" shouted a man near the Browns. "More! More!"

Paddington gave the man a hard stare as he stepped out of the bucket.

He'd had quite enough of being a trapeze artist for one night.

Even the Ring-master had to admit that
Paddington had been the star turn of the
evening, and at the end of the show he gave him
another ice-cream and insisted he took part in
the Grand Parade.

"It's a pity we're only here for one night," he
said sadly. "I'd like to have you in my circus all
the time."

"Do you still want to join a circus, Paddington?" asked Judy, later that night.

Paddington shook his head. And then a faraway look came into his eyes as he tested his sheets carefully to make sure he was safely tucked in.

"But it was *very* nice to be asked," he said. "I don't suppose there are many bears from Darkest Peru who can say they've been on a trapeze!"

Paddington
Goes Shopping

One day, not long after Paddington went to live with the Browns at number thirty-two Windsor Gardens, Mrs Brown thought she would take him out shopping.

"We're going to the Portobello Road," explained
Judy. "It's a big market quite near here."

"I should bring your pocket money," added
Jonathan. "There's a lot to see."

Paddington didn't need asking twice and soon afterwards they all set off.

Suddenly they turned a corner and he found himself in what seemed like a different world: a

world of shops and street barrows, gold and silver ornaments, books, old furniture, fruit and vegetables, people . . . his eyes grew larger and larger as he tried to take it all in.

One shop was even having its photograph taken.
"That's a new supermarket," explained Judy.
"There must be something special on."
Paddington's mouth began to water as he

peered through the glass. "Perhaps I could do some shopping for you, Mrs Brown?" he said hopefully.

Mrs Brown hesitated. She wasn't at all sure about letting him go off on his own quite so soon, but Jonathan told her not to worry.

"Even Paddington can't get lost in a supermarket," he said. "What goes in must come out."

"We can meet him by the cash desk on our way back," added Judy.

Paddington felt most important as he entered the shop.

He lifted his hat to the manager, who was standing just inside the door, and then consulted Mrs Brown's shopping list.

Everywhere he looked there were shelves piled high with packets and tins. There was even one shelf with nothing but marmalade, so he could quite see why it was called a *super*market.

His paws were soon full and he was just
beginning to wish he'd left his suitcase at home
when he saw the manager coming towards him
pushing a large basket on wheels.

"May I suggest you have one of these, sir?"
he called.

"You can take as much as you want now," he continued.

"Can I really?" exclaimed Paddington.

The manager nodded. "Yes, we like to make

our customers happy."

Paddington looked most impressed. "In that case," he said, "I think I'll have *two* baskets – just to make sure."

The more Paddington saw of the supermarket
the more he liked it, and he felt sure Mrs Brown
would be pleased when she saw all her free
groceries.

The other customers looked on in amazement. "Perhaps he's trying to win an eating prize," suggested one lady, as he went past, his baskets laden with goods.

But the customers weren't the only ones who were watching Paddington with interest.

Since he had been in the shop the manager had been joined by several other important looking men, and as he reached the cash desk one of them gave a signal, and they all started to clap.

Paddington had never been in a shop where
they tried so hard to make their customers
happy, and he gave the men a friendly wave as
he unloaded his baskets.

"Well done!" said the lady, handing him a
ticket. "I hope you've brought a lorry with you.
There's over fifty pounds' worth here!"

Paddington stared at the long roll of paper in his paw.

"*Over fifty pounds' worth*!" he gasped, hardly able to believe his eyes or his ears.

Giving the man who had said he could take as much as he wanted one of his hardest ever stares, he opened his suitcase and peered inside.

"But I've only got threepence!"

Looking up, Paddington suddenly caught sight
of a crowd of people coming towards him.

"Watch out!" cried the lady as he made a
grab for his shopping.

But it was too late. With a roar like an express
train the whole lot began to tumble down off the
counter.

126

Paddington was still sitting on the floor covered with groceries when the Browns rushed into the shop to see what was going on.

All in all he decided he was much safer where he was for the time being.

"You wouldn't think," said the manager, "that giving someone a prize would be so difficult."

"A *prize*?" echoed the Browns. The manager pointed to a large notice on the wall.

"This young bear," he said, "happens to be our thousandth customer today. Perhaps you'd like to tell him he's won a free supply of groceries!"

"All of which," said Judy, as they staggered
home laden with shopping, "only goes to
show that bears always fall on their feet."

"Even in supermarkets!" agreed Jonathan.

Paddington sniffed the air happily. "I like the
Portobello Road," he said. "I think I shall
always do my shopping here from now on."

Paddington
at the Tower

Soon after Paddington went to live at number thirty-two Windsor Gardens Mr and Mrs Brown gave him a basket on wheels.

The Browns' house was near the Portobello Road,

where there was a large market, and every
morning Paddington went there to do his shopping.

After calling at the baker's, where he had a
standing order for buns, he then went on to see
his friend Mr Gruber, who kept an antique shop.

Paddington liked Mr Gruber's shop. It was so full of things it was like Aladdin's cave.

Every day Mr Gruber made some cocoa and they had their "elevenses" together.

One morning, however, Paddington had a
surprise. When he reached the shop he found Mr
Gruber busy putting up his shutters.

"It's Easter Monday, Mr Brown," he said.

"And as it's such a nice day I thought I would tak

you and Jonathan and Judy on a mystery outing."

Paddington was very excited. He hurried back home to tell the others and then he began making some marmalade sandwiches. He soon had so many he could hardly close the lid of his suitcase.

Later that morning they set off, and Mr Gruber
found them a seat right at the front of the bus so
that he could point out the interesting sights on
the way.

They had been travelling for quite a while

when Jonathan and Judy suddenly let out a cry.

"I know where we're going," said Judy, as they turned a corner.

"It's the Tower of London!" exclaimed Jonathan.

Paddington had never been to the Tower of
London before and he was most impressed. It
was much, much bigger than he had pictured.
As they reached the entrance a man in a

strange uniform stepped forward to take their
tickets.

"That's one of the Beefeaters," whispered
Jonathan. "They look after the Tower."

"They're really Yeomen Warders," explained Judy. "But they get called Beefeaters because in the old days they used to taste all the Royal food to make sure it was safe to eat."

Paddington raised his hat politely and then opened his suitcase.

"Would you like one of my marmalade sandwiches?" he asked. "I expect it will make a nice change from beef."

"A *marmalade sandwich*!" spluttered the Beefeater. He held the object up between his thumb and forefinger and stared at it as if he could hardly believe his eyes.

But when he looked down again Paddington had gone.

Taking one look at the expression on the man's face, he picked up his suitcase and hurried after the others. Several more sandwiches dropped out on the way, but by then he was much too upset to notice.

Mr Gruber hastily led them through an arch. When they were safely round the corner he stopped beside a large cage.

"This is where they keep the ravens, Mr Brown," he said.

"They've always had ravens here and it's said that if they ever fly away, then the Tower will fall down."

Paddington peered at the empty cage. "Perhaps we'd better go soon, Mr Gruber," he said anxiously.

Mr Gruber laughed. "I don't think there's any fear of it happening just yet, Mr Brown," he said. "That Tower looks very solid to me."

He pointed towards a large black bird standing watching them. "Besides, there's at least one raven keeping an eye on things."

"He looks as if he's got his eye on Paddington," said Judy.

Next, Mr Gruber took them to a room deep under the ground.

"This is where the Crown Jewels are kept," whispered Judy. "They are made of gold and they are very valuable. That's why they are kept behind glass."

Mr Gruber showed them the St Edward's Crown

. . . the Orb and Sceptre

. . . and an Ampula and Spoon for holy oil.

"They were all used by the Queen at her Coronation," he explained. "The crown has over four hundred precious stones and it weighs nearly five pounds!"

Paddington's eyes grew larger and larger. He could quite see why no-one wanted the Tower to fall down.

When they came out of the Jewel House
Paddington noticed a strange thing. There were
now two ravens watching him.

A moment later two more arrived, and all four
stared at him as he went past.

Paddington gave them a hard stare back, but for once it didn't seem to have any effect.

"Perhaps we'd better have our picnic outside by the river," said Judy, when she saw the worried look on Paddington's face. "They won't follow you out there."

But the ravens did follow Paddington, and by
the time they reached the gate there were so
many he'd nearly lost count.

"And where do you think you are going with our ravens, young fellow-me-bear?" asked the Beefeater in charge.

"*He's* not going anywhere with them," said Jonathan and Judy. "*They're* going with him."

"It makes no difference," said the man sternly. "I'm not letting them leave here and risk having the place fall down. That bear will have to stay in the Tower until we've decided what's best."

"Oh, crikey!" groaned Jonathan. "Fancy Paddington being sent to the Tower."

Suddenly Mr Gruber had an idea. "You know
what?" he said excitedly. "I don't think it's Mr
Brown they're after at all. I think it's his
sandwiches!"

Paddington gazed at Mr Gruber in astonishment.
"My sandwiches!" he exclaimed hotly.

But Mr Gruber was right. Sure enough, as
soon as Paddington opened his suitcase all the
ravens gathered round and began pecking at the
contents.

"All the years I've been here," said the Beefeater,
"and I never knew ravens like marmalade."
He looked at Paddington with new respect.
"Perhaps you could give me your address, sir.

Then if any of our birds ever get lost we can
send for you.

"We may even be able to find you a special
jar of marmalade to keep by you in case it's
needed in a hurry."

"Trust Paddington to get sent to the Tower and then end up with a jar of marmalade!" exclaimed Judy.

Paddington looked at it happily. "If I'm to be a Marmalade-eater," he announced, "perhaps I'd better test it now – just to make sure!"

Paddington at the Sea-side

"Today," said Mr Brown at breakfast one bright, summer morning, "feels like the kind of day for taking a young bear to the sea-side. Hands up all those who agree."

Jonathan, Judy and Mrs Brown all put up their hands.

And Paddington raised both of his paws as well, just to make sure.

Everyone was very excited, and by the time they set out the Browns' car was so full of things there was hardly room to move.

Paddington carefully fastened his safety belt, and then peered out of the window as he felt the car turn a corner.

"Are we nearly there, Mr Brown?" he asked hopefully.

Mr Brown removed a spade handle from his left ear. "I'm afraid not," he said gloomily. "We've only just left Windsor Gardens, and it's a very long way to the sea."

Mr Brown was right. It *was* a long journey. But when they reached the sea-side the sight of the sand and the water soon made up for it.

Paddington gave an excited sniff as he climbed out of the car. Even the air had a different smell.

"That's because it's special sea-side air," said Mrs Brown. "It's very good for you."

Paddington looked round anxiously as Mr Brown
began laying out the beach things.

"I hope all the air doesn't get used up, Mrs
Brown," he said in a loud voice. And he gave a
man who was doing some deep-breathing
exercises a very hard stare indeed.

"Come on, Paddington," called Judy. "Let's go for a swim."

It took Paddington some while to get ready. He wasn't the sort of bear who believed in taking chances and by the time he went in the sea he was wearing so many things he promptly sank.

"No wonder!" cried Judy, as she went to his rescue. "You haven't even bothered to blow up your paw-bands!"

"Fancy wearing a duffle-coat!" exclaimed Jonathan.

"I thought the water might be cold," gasped Paddington.

After his paw-bands had been properly blown up Paddington went in the water again, and with some help from Jonathan and Judy he was soon swimming very well indeed.

After his swim Paddington settled down in a deckchair in order to dry out.

He had hardly closed his eyes when he heard
something very strange going on behind him.

First there was a loud cry.

Then there was the sound of people booing.

"They're watching Mr Briggs' Punch and
Judy," explained Mrs Brown.

Paddington jumped up and looked at the others as if he could hardly believe his ears. But Mr and Mrs Brown seemed much too busy with the picnic things to be bothered, so he turned and hurried up the beach towards the spot where the noise was coming from.

"Where's Paddington?" asked Jonathan, when he and Judy arrived back shortly afterwards carrying some ice-creams.

"I hope he's not long," said Judy. "I've got him a special giant cone. He'll be most upset if it all melts."

Jonathan glanced up and down the beach. "Crikey!" he said suddenly. "Look over there!"

The Browns gave a gasp as they turned to follow the direction of Jonathan's gaze.

Something very odd seemed to be going on inside the Punch and Judy tent.

There was a large bulge in one side and it was heaving up and down almost as if it was alive.

Suddenly the tent began moving across the sand, scattering people in all directions. It just missed a large sand-castle, went twice round the ice-cream man, and then headed towards the sea.

"Quick!" shouted Judy. "Let's cut it off!"

But she was too late.

"Paddington!" cried Judy, as a familiar figure swam into view. "What on earth are you doing? That's the second time I've had to rescue you!"

Paddington stared at her in amazement. "But I went to rescue *you*!" he exclaimed. "Mrs Brown said you were being punched by Mr Briggs."

Mrs Brown looked at Paddington in astonishment. Then her face cleared.

"I didn't say Mr Briggs was *punching* Judy," she explained. "I said it was his Punch *and* Judy."

"It's a puppet theatre," said Judy. "They often have them at the sea-side. There's one puppet called Mr Punch, and when he gets cross all the audience have to boo."

If it took the Browns a long time to explain a Punch and Judy show to Paddington, it took them even longer to explain Paddington to Mr Briggs.

But when he saw the enormous crowd watching them from the promenade his face lit up. It was the biggest audience he'd had for a long time and he decided to make the most of it and put another show on there and then.

"You can have a seat in the front row," he said to Paddington. "I expect bears do very good boos."

One way and another Paddington enjoyed his day
out at the sea-side. But all good things come
to an end, and when it was time to leave he stood
for a moment holding up an empty marmalade jar.

"I'm just collecting some sea air for the journey
home," he announced.

"I think I shall sleep so well on the way back
I may lose all of today's air with my snores!"